I would like to dedicate this book to my grandparents, Getrude Ebanks, who is 85 years young, and the late Lowel Ebanks. Granny, thank you for your soothing musical voice. Papa, thank you for sharing your stories. Your legacy will continue. My children, Nikeisha and Nathan, thanks for encouraging me to tell you stories over and over again. My grandson, Jeremiah, everything imaginable is within your reach. Andrea, thank you for the "action plan." It worked.

Kafiya meets the Moon

Janet Campbell

Illustrated by Anais Lee

Kafiya Johnson lived with her mother, Grandma Etta, and Auntie Yaya in a country home outside of the city. Their home was surrounded by a lot of apple trees. Kafiya loved living there. She especially liked the summer when the apples turned from green to maroon and then a brilliant fire red.

But there was something Kafiya liked more than anything. Whenever there was a full moon, Kafiya loved taking walks with her Grandma Etta. Grandma Etta often told her, "Whenever you see a full moon, child, remember that you have its full attention. The moon sees and hears everything."

The moon was a mystery to Kafiya, but for now, she was content taking walks, playing with her shadow, and singing her favorite song, a song that Grandma Etta taught her:

Shadow, shadow, where is my shadow?
Up in the tree, where it can be free?
Or hiding behind those apple trees?
Wherever you are, shadow
Come back to me,
Come back to me.

As Kafiya got older, she became more and more curious about the moon and about seeing her shadow by moonlight. She wondered why sometimes she would see a full moon but other times only a half or quarter moon. She had many questions about the moon and these questions kept her busy looking for answers.

Kafiya asked her friends if they knew anything about the moon. They often laughed and made fun of her fascination with the moon.

One night when Kafiya was taking a walk with her mother and playing with her shadow, she asked, "Mommy, can you tell me about the moon?" For what seemed like a long time, her mother said nothing. But Kafiya waited patiently, looking up at her mother's face and thinking how beautiful she looked in the moonlight.

"The moon," said her mother slowly, "is God's creation. We should just admire its mystery." Kafiya walked quietly beside her mother. "You hearing me, child?" her mother said.

"Yes, Mommy," said Kafiya, though she was not satisfied with the answer. "Is that what Grandma Etta told you?"

"I don't remember," her mother said a bit impatiently. "Why, child, do you ask so many questions?"

Kafiya was troubled by her mother's answer, and she comforted herself by singing her favorite song:

Shadow, shadow, where is my shadow?
Up in the tree, where it can be free?
Or hiding behind those apple trees?
Wherever you are, shadow
Come back to me,
Come back to me.

Still determined to get answers to her questions, Kafiya decided to go to her Auntie Yaya. Her aunt did love to talk, and she was more patient with Kafiya than her mother. One night, she sat quietly beside her aunt on the front porch, watching the apple tree dance under the moonlight.

"Auntie, tell me about the moon."

Her aunt pulled her close and said, "I'll tell you what I know. It's what your Grandma Etta and her mother before her told me." Auntie Yaya's voice was soft and smooth as butter. "The moon is God's creation, and since it's that, we should just admire it. There is a face in the moon, your Grandma Etta once told me. So that moon up there can see and hear everything. Some say it can even talk."

"There's a face in the moon! And it can talk!" Kafiya said excitedly.

Auntie Yaya continued, "When I was a little girl in the Caribbean, at the full moon, people in our town would gather under a tree. Children like you would play ring games, sing songs, and old people would tell stories long into the night. A few stories would start with this chant: 'Cry, cry, baby, moonshine darling, take off your shoes and go to bed.'"

"But what does that mean, Auntie?"

"Well, for one thing, it let the children know that the story might be a scary one. And sometimes the younger ones would be sent to bed, but the older ones would stay to hear the stories."

"And did they really tell stories all night long?"

"Of course not, Kafiya," Auntie Yaya laughed. "But at the end of the storytelling, some of the children would look up to the moon and yell, 'Look! Look! There's a face in the moon!' and we would all look up and admire that face."

That night in bed, Kafiya prayed that she would meet the moon face-to-face. Thereafter, she watched the moon each night from her bedroom window. As the half-moon became larger, her excitement grew, and she became impatient for the next full moon.

One night, there it was in the starry sky. As she sat on the front porch looking at it, it seemed to be closer than it had been in the past. She spoke to the moon in a very soft voice, saying, "Moon, do you have eyes like me?"

Suddenly, she could see the moon's eyes. She stared and stared at them, then asked, "Moon, do you have a nose like me?"

And there was the nose, just like that.

Feeling bolder now, she said, "You have a mouth like me, don't you?"

And the mouth appeared.

Out of the silence, a great big voice boomed, "Kafiya Johnson, you are a very brave and curious little girl, and I like that."

Kafiya tried to speak to the moon, but she couldn't find her voice. Questions jumped around her head. *Where did the moon get its beautiful light?* She wanted to ask, but the words wouldn't leave her mouth. She touched her fingers to her lips, telling the moon that she couldn't speak.

The moon said, "I know, Kafiya, I know all the questions you would like to ask me. By the end of my visit, I'll answer everything. I promise."

Kafiya sat quietly while the moon began to tell her story.

"As you know, my name is Moon. I live in the sky with my family. In the daytime, my older sister, Sun, lights up the earth. My younger sisters, all called Stars, light up the sky, most nights, anyway. My sisters and I were meant to light up the sky, but once I was born, my parents knew I could never do this without the help of my older sister, Sun."

Spellbound, Kafiya listened. After some time, she said, "I can't believe the moon is actually talking to me."

The moon went on, "My parents told me that I am like a mirror, for one part of me is always dark, and the other part, where Sun shines, is bright. People on Earth only see the part of me lit up by my sister."

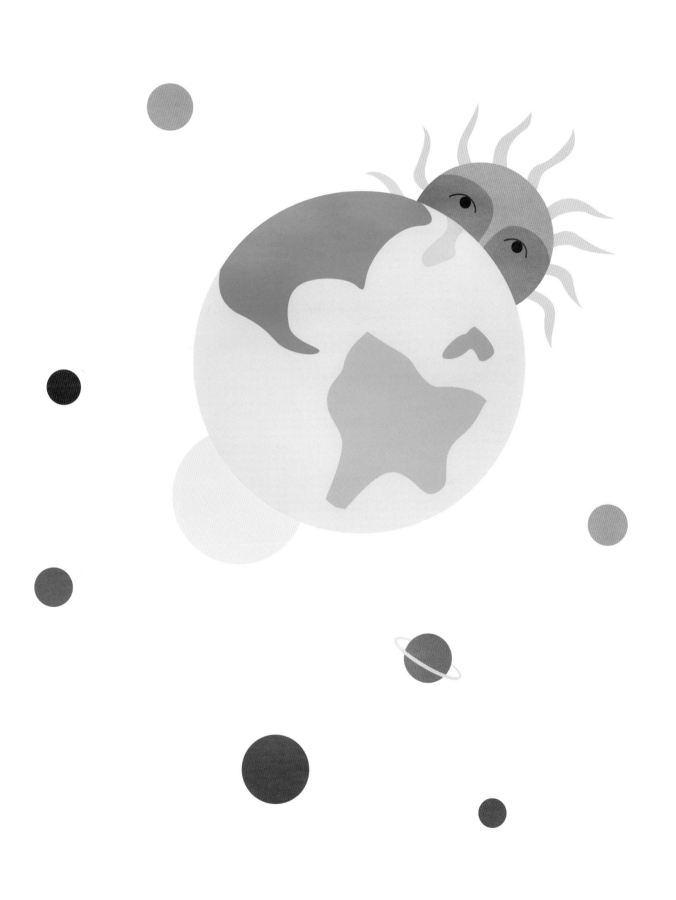

"I'm constantly moving around the earth, visiting places, and talking to children, so Sun has a hard time keeping me lit. That's why my shape is always changing. Sometimes, you can see all of me, like tonight, and then people call me the full moon. Other times, you can see only half or even just a quarter of me."

By the time Moon had finished her story, Kafiya had found her voice. She was about to thank her, but in a flash, Moon returned to the sky to be with her sisters. So Kafiya went into the house, went to her mother's room, and told her about Moon's visit. Her mother just smiled and said, "Go to bed, child. Your imagination is too wild."

Too excited to sleep, Kafiya headed for her Auntie Yaya's room. "Auntie Yaya, you were right! The moon does have eyes! And a nose! And a mouth!"

"Nonsense, child," her auntie laughed. "Go to bed. We'll talk in the morning."

Kafiya turned away and shook her head. Who could she tell? Who would take her seriously? After a moment, she went into Grandma Etta's room and sat beside her. "Grandma Etta," she said, "I want you to listen to me, but you can't laugh. Promise?"

Grandma Etta promised to listen to her and not laugh.

When Kafiya finished her story, she looked at Grandma Etta and said, "Do you believe me?"

"Of course, my little Kafiya. I believe you because when I was your age, the moon spoke to me."

Kafiya thanked Grandma Etta for believing her, then kissed her goodnight, and hurried to her room.

She sat on her bed, admiring the moon and her sisters, though just now, they seemed far away. She would always remember this night. Wrapping a light cotton sheet around her shoulders, softly she began to sing.

Shadow, shadow, where is my shadow?
Up in the tree, where it can be free?
Or hiding behind those apple trees?
Wherever you are, shadow
Come back to me,
Come back to me.

Then, as moonlight streamed through her window, she saw her shadow playing hide-and-seek among her family's apple trees.

The End

This is Janet Campbell's first book. Janet has practiced the art of storytelling and sharing folktales her entire life. Her passion for storytelling grew when she saw the tradition was dying. After using storytelling for years in her community work to bridge cultural gaps, the transition to writing was inevitable for Janet. Janet was born in St. Catherine, Jamaica, but has called Canada her home for over thirty years. Janet is the owner of Nanni's Natural Hair Salon.

To learn more about Janet and her future projects, please visit www.janetcampbell.ca or look for her on Facebook under "Telling Your Tales."

Have a book idea?

Contact us at:

Mascot Books
560 Herndon Parkway
Suite 120
Herndon, VA 20170

info@mascotbooks.com | www.mascotbooks.com